Cerberus,
The Dog of Hades

Maurice Bloomfield

Contents

CERBERUS,
THE DOG OF HADES

BY

Maurice Bloomfield

To the Memory
of
F. Max Mueller

CERBERUS, THE DOG OF HADES

Hermes, the guide of the dead, brings to Pluto's kingdom their psyches, "that gibber like bats, as they fare down the dank ways, past the streams of Okeanos, past the gates of the sun and the land of dreams, to the meadow of asphodel in the dark realm of Hades, where dwell the souls, the phantoms of men outworn." So begins the twenty-fourth book of the *Odyssey*. Later poets have Charon, a grim boatsman, receive the dead at the River of Woe; he ferries them across, provided the passage money has been placed in their mouths, and their bodies have been duly buried in the world above. Otherwise they are left to gibber on the hither bank. Pluto's house, wide-gated, thronged with guests, has a janitor Kerberos, sometimes friendly, sometimes snarling when new guests arrive, but always hostile to those who would depart. Honey cakes are provided for them that are about to go to Hades--the sop to Cerberus. This dog, nameless and undescribed, Homer mentions simply as the dog of Hades, whom Herakles, as the last and chief test of his strength, snatched from the horrible house of Hades.[1] First Hesiod and next Stesichorus discover his name to be Kerberos. The latter seems to have composed a poem on the dog. Hesiod[2] mentions not only the name but also the genealogy of Kerberos. Of Typhaon and Echidna he was born, the irresistible and ineffable flesh-devourer, the voracious, brazen-voiced, fifty-headed dog of hell.

Plato in the *Republic* refers to the composite nature of Kerberos.[3] Not until Apollodorus (2. 5. 12. 1. ff.), in the second century B. C., comes the familiar description: Kerberos now has three dog heads, a dragon tail, and his back is covered with the heads of serpents. But his plural heads must have been familiarly assumed by the Greeks; this will appear from the evidence of their sculptures and vase-paintings.

CERBERUS IN CLASSIC ART.

Classic art has taken up Cerberus very generously; his treatment, however, is far from being as definite as that of the Greek and Roman poets. Statues, sarcophagi, and vase paintings whose theme is Hades, or scenes laid in Hades, represent him as a ferocious Greek collie, often encircled with serpents, and with a serpent for a tail, but there is no certainty as to the number of his heads. Often he is three-headed in art as in literature, as may be seen conveniently in the reproductions in Baumeister's *Denkmaeler des Klassischen Altertums*. Very familiar is the statue in the villa Borghese of Pluto enthroned, three-headed Cerberus by his side.[4] A Greek scarabaeus shows a pair of lovers, or a married couple, who have died at the same time, crossing in Charon's ferry. As they are approaching the other bank of the Styx, where a three-headed Cerberus is awaiting them, the girl seems afright and is upheld by her male companion.[5] On the other hand, a bronze in Naples shows the smiling boy Herakles engaged in strangling two serpents, one with each hand. The figure rests on a cylindrical base upon which are depicted eight of the wonderful deeds which Herakles performs later on. By a rope he leads a *two-headed* Cerberus from Hades.[6] This last of the wonderful deeds of Herakles is a favorite theme of vase pictures. Herakles is regularly accompanied by Hermes and Athena; the dog, whose marvelous shape Homer fails to reveal, is generally two-headed. Such a vase may be seen in Gerhard, *Auserlesene Vasenbilder*, ii. 131. [7] Or still more conveniently, Professor Norton has reproduced[8] an amphora in the Louvre with a picture of the dicephalous Kerberos. Upon the forehead of each of the two heads rises a serpent. Herakles in tunic and lion's skin, armed with bow, quiver, and sword, stoops towards the dog. He holds a chain in his left hand, while he stretches out his right with a petting gesture. Between the two is a tree, against which leans the club of Herakles. Behind him stands Athena.

CERBERUS IN ROMAN AND MODERN LITERATURE.

Neither Greek literature, nor Greek art, however, really seems to fix either the shape or nature of Kerberos; it was left to the Roman poets to say the last word about him. They finally settle the number of his heads, or the number of his bodies fused in one. He is *triceps* "three-headed," *triplex* or *tergeminus* "threefold," *triformis* "of three bodies," or simply Tricerberus. Tibullus says explicitly that he has both three heads and three tongues: *cui tres sint linguae tergeminumque caput*. Virgil, in the *AEneid*, vi. 417, has huge Cerberus barking with triple jaws; his neck bristles with serpents. Ovid in his *Metamorphoses*, x. 21, makes Orpheus, looking for dear Eurydice in Tartarus, declare that he did not go down in order that he might chain the three necks, shaggy with serpents, of the monster begotten of Medusa. His business also is settled for all time; he is the terrible, fearless, and watchful janitor, or guardian (janitor or *custos*) of Orcus, the Styx, Lethe, or the black Kingdom.[9] And so he remains for modern poets, as when Dante, reproducing Virgil, describes him:[10]

"When Cerberus, that great worm, had seen us   His mouth he opened and his fangs were shown,   And then my leader with his folded palms   Took of the earth, and filling full his hand,   Into those hungry gullets flung it down."

Or Shakespeare, *Love's Labor Lost*, v. ii: "Great Hercules is presented by this imp whose club killed Cerberus, the three-headed *canis*."

CLASSICAL EXPLANATIONS OF CERBERUS.

Such classical explanations of Cerberus' shape as I have seen are feeble and foolishly reasonable. Heraclitus, [Greek: Peri apiston] 331, states that Kerberos had two pups. They always attended their father, and therefore he appeared to be three-headed. The mythographer Palaephatos(39) states that Kerberos was considered three-headed from his name [Greek: Trikarenos] which he obtained from the city Trikarenos in Phliasia. And a late Roman rationalistic mythographer by the name of Fulgentius[11] tells us that Petronius defined Cerberus as the lawyer of Hades, apparently because of his three jaws, or the cumulative glibness of three tongues. Fulgentius himself has a ***fabula*** in which he says that Cerberus means ***Creaboros***, that is, "flesh-eating," and that the three heads of Cerberus are respectively, infancy, youth, and old age, through which death has entered the circle of the earth--per quas introivit mors in orbem terrarum.[12]

A MODERN VIEW.

"Lasciate ogni speranza voi ch' entrate"

Can we bid this "schwankende Gestalt," this monstrous vision, floating about upon the filmy photographs of murky Hades, stand still, emerge into light, and assume clear and reasonable outlines?

"Hence loathed melancholy of Cerberus and blackest Midnight born."

An American humorist, John Kendrick Bangs, who likes to place his skits in Hades, steps in "where angels fear to tread," and launches with a light heart the discussion as to whether Cerberus is one or more dogs. The city of Cimmeria in Hades, having tried asphalt pavement, which was found too sloppy for that climate, and Nicholson wood pavement, which kept taking fire, decides on Belgian blocks. In order to meet the new expense a dog-tax is imposed. Since Cerberus belongs to Hades as a whole, the state must pay his tax, and is willing enough to do so--on Cerberus as one dog. The city, however, endeavors to collect on three dogs--one license for each head. Two infernal coppers, sent to impound Cerberus, fare not well, one of them being badly chewed up by Cerberus, the other nabbed bodily and thrown into the Styx. In consequence of this they obtain damages from the city. The city then decides to bring suit against the state. The bench consists of Apollyon himself and Judge Blackstone; Coke appears for the city, Catiline for the state. The first dog-catcher, called to testify, and asked whether he is familiar with dogs, replies in the affirmative, adding that he had never got quite so intimate with one as he got with him.

"With whom?" asks Coke.

"Cerberus," replies the witness.

"Do you consider him to be one dog, two dogs, or three dogs?"

Catiline objects to this question as a leading one, but Coke manages to get it in under another form: "How many dogs did you see when you saw Cerberus?"

"Three, anyhow," replies the witness with feeling, "though afterwards I thought there was a whole bench-show atop of me."

On cross-examination Catiline asks him blandly: "My poor friend, if you considered Cerberus to be three dogs anyhow, why did you in your examination a moment since refer to the avalanche of caninity, of which you so affectingly speak, as him?"

"He is a him," sturdily says the witness. After this Coke, discomfited, decides to call his second witness: "What is your business?" asks Coke, after the usual preliminaries.

"I'm out of business. Livin' on my damages."

"What damages?"

"Them I got from the city for injuries did me by that there--I should say them there--dorgs, Cerberus."

And so on. Catiline gains the day for the state by his superior logic; the city of Cimmeria must content itself with taxes on a single dog. But the logic of the facts, it will appear, are with the dog-catchers, Judge Coke, and the city of Cimmeria as against the state of Hades: Cerberus is more than one dog.

FUTURE LIFE IN THE VEDA.

India is the home of the Cerberus myth in its clearest and fullest development. In order to appreciate its nature we must bear in mind that the early Hindu conceptions of a future life are auspicious, and quite the reverse of sombre. The statements in the Veda about life after death exclude all notions of hell. The early visions are simple, poetic and cheerful. The bodies of the dead are burned and their ashes are consigned to earth. But this is viewed merely as a symbolic act of preparation--cooking it is called forthright--for another life of joy. The righteous forefathers of old who died before, they have found another good place. Especially Yama, the first mortal, has gone to the great rivers on high; he has searched out, like a pioneer, the way for all his descendants: "He went before and found a dwelling which no power can debar us from. Our fathers of old have traveled the path; it leads every earth-born mortal thither. There in the midst of the highest heaven beams unfading light and eternal waters flow; there every wish is fulfilled on the rich meadows of Yama." Day by day Yama sends forth two dogs, his messengers, to search out among men those who are to join the fathers that are having an excellent time in Yama's company.

THE TWO DOGS OF YAMA.

The tenth book of the ***Rig-Veda*** contains in hymns 14-18 a collection of funeral stanzas quite unrivaled for mythological and ethnological interest in the literature of ancient peoples. In hymn 14 there are three stanzas (10-12) that deal with the two dogs of Yama. This is the classical passage, all depends upon its interpretation. They contain detached statements which take up the idea from different points of view, that are not easily harmonized as long as the dogs are merely ordinary canines; they resolve themselves fitly and neatly into a pair of natural objects, if we follow closely all the ideas which the Hindus associated with them.

In the first place, it is clear that we are dealing with the conception of Cerberus. In stanza 10 the two dogs are conceived as ill-disposed creatures, standing guard to keep the departed souls out of bliss. The soul on its way to heaven is addressed as follows:

"Run past straightway the two four-eyed dogs, the spotted and (the dark), the brood of Saram[=a]; enter in among the propitious fathers who hold high feast with Yama."

A somewhat later text, the book of house-rite of [=A]cval[=a]yana, has the notion of the sop to Cerberus: "To the two dogs born in the house of (Yama) Vivasvant's son, to the dark and the spotted, I have given a cake; do ye guard me ever on my road!"

The twelfth stanza of the ***Rig-Veda*** hymn strikes a somewhat different note which suggests both good and evil in the character of the two dogs: "The two brown, broad-nosed messengers of Yama, life-robbing, wander among men. May they restore to us to-day the auspicious breath of life, that we may behold the sun." Evidently the part of the Cerberi here is not in harmony with their function in stanza 10: instead of debarring men from the abodes of bliss they pick out the dead that are ultimately destined to boon companionship with Yama. The same idea is expressed simply and clearly in prayers for long life in the ***Atharva-Veda***: "The two dogs of Yama, the dark and the spotted, that guard the road (to heaven), that have been dispatched, shall not (go after) thee! Come hither, do not long to be away! Do not tarry here with thy mind turned to a distance." (viii. 1. 9.) And again: "Remain here, O man, with thy soul entire! Do not follow the two messengers of Yama; come to the abodes of the living." (v. 30. 6.)

These prayers contain the natural, yet under the circumstances rather paradoxical, desire to live yet a little longer upon the earth in the light of the sun. Fitfully the mortal Hindu regales himself with saccharine promises of paradise; in his every-day mood he clings to life and shrinks with the uneasy sense that his paradise may not materialize, even if the hope is expressed glibly and fluently. The real craving is expressed in numberless passages: "May we live a hundred autumns, surrounded by lusty sons." Homer's Hades has wiped out this inconsistency, only to substitute another. Odysseus, on returning from his visit to Hades, exclaims baldly: "Better a swineherd on the surface of the earth in the light of the sun than king of the shades in Hades." It is almost adding insult to injury to have the road to such a Hades barred by Cerberus. This latter paradox must be removed in order that the myth shall become intelligible.

The eleventh of the ***Rig-Veda*** stanzas presents the two dogs as guides of the soul [Greek: psychopompoi] to heaven: "To thy two four-eyed, road-guarding, man-beholding watch-dogs entrust him, O King Yama, and bestow on him prosperity and health."

THE TWO DOGS IN HEAVEN.

With the change of the abode of the dead from inferno to heaven the two Cerberi are *eo ipso* also evicted. That follows of itself, even if we had not explicit testimony. A legend of the Br[=a]hmana-texts, the Hindu equivalent of the Talmud, tells repeatedly that there are two dogs *in heaven*, and that these two dogs are Yama's dogs. I shall present two versions of the story, a kind of [Greek: Gigantomachia] in order to establish the equation between the terms "two dogs of Yama," and "two heavenly dogs."

"There were Asuras (demons) named K[=a]lak[=a]njas. They piled up a fire altar in order to obtain the world of heaven. Man by man they placed a brick upon it. The god Indra, passing himself off for a Brahmin, put on a brick for himself. They climbed up to heaven. Indra pulled out his brick; they tumbled down. And they who tumbled down became spiders; two flew up, and became the two heavenly dogs." (Br[=a]hmana of the T[=a]ittir[=i]yas 1. 1. 2.)

"The Asuras (demons) called K[=a]lak[=a]njas piled bricks for an altar, saying: 'We will ascend to heaven.' Indra, passing himself off for a Brahmin, came to them; he put on a brick. They at first came near getting to heaven; then Indra tore out his brick. The Asuras becoming quite feeble fell down; the two that were uppermost became the dogs of Yama, those which were lower became spiders." (Br[=a]hmana of the M[=a]itra 1. 6. 9.)

This theme is so well fixed in the minds of the time that it is elaborated in a charm to preserve from some kind of injury, addressed to the mythic figures of the legend:

"Through the air he flies looking down upon all beings: with the majesty of the heavenly dog, with that oblation would we pay homage to thee.

"The three K[=a]lak[=a]njas, that are fixed upon the sky like gods, all these I have called to help, to render this person free from harm.

"In the waters is thy origin, upon the heavens thy home, in the middle of the sea, and upon the earth, thy greatness; with the majesty of the heavenly dog, with that oblation would we pay homage to thee." (Atharva-Veda vi., 80.)

The single heavenly dog that is described here is of no mean interest. The passage proves the individual character of each of the two dogs of Yama; they cannot be a vague pair of heavenly dogs, but must be based each upon some definite phenomenon in the heavens.

Yet another text, Hiranyakecin's book of house-rites, locates the dogs of Yama, describing them in unmistakable language, in heaven: "The brood of Saram[=a], dark beneath and brown, run, looking down upon the sea." (ii. 7. 2.)

THE TWO DOGS OF YAMA EXPLAIN THEMSELVES.

T here are not many things in heaven that can be represented as a pair, coursing across the sky, looking down upon the sea, and having other related properties. My readers will make a shrewd guess, but I prefer to let the texts themselves unfold the transparent mystery. The Veda of the **Katha** school (xxxvii. 14) says: "These two dogs of Yama, verily, are day and night," and the Br[=a]hmana of the K[=a]ush[=i]takins (ii. 9) argues in Talmudic strain: "At eve, when the sun has gone down, before darkness has set in, one should sacrifice the **agnihotra**-sacrifice; in the morning before sunrise, when darkness is dispelled, at that time, one should sacrifice the **agnihotra**-sacrifice; at that time the gods arrive. Therefore (the two dogs of Yama) Cy[=a]ma and Cabala (the dark and the spotted) tear to pieces the **agnihotra** of him that sacrifices otherwise. Cabala is the day; Cy[=a]ma is the night. He who sacrifices in the night, his **agnihotra** Cy[=a]ma tears asunder; he who sacrifices in broad daylight, his **agnihotra** Cabala tears asunder." Even more drily the two dogs of Yama are correlated with the time-markers of heaven in a passage of the T[=a]ittir[=i]ya-Veda (v. 7. 19); here sundry parts of the sacrificial horse are assigned to four cosmic phenomena in the following order: 1. Sun and moon. 2. Cy[=a]ma and Cabala (the two dogs of Yama). 3. Dawn. 4. Evening twilight. So that the dogs of Yama are sandwiched in between sun and moon on the one side, dawn and evening twilight on the other. Obviously they are here, either as a special designation of day and night, or their physical equivalents, sun and moon. And now the Catapatha-Br[=a]hmana says explicitly: "The moon verily is the divine dog; he looks down upon the cattle of the sacrificer." And again a passage in the Kashmir version of the **Atharva-Veda** says: "The four-eyed dog (the moon) surveys by night the sphere of the night."

SUN AND MOON AS STATIONS ON THE WAY TO SALVATION.

Even the theosophic Upanishads are compelled to make their way through this tolerably crude mythology when they come to deal with the passage of the soul to release from existence and absorption in the universal Brahma. The human mind does not easily escape some kind of eschatological topography. The Brahma itself may be devoid of all properties, universal, pervasive, situated below as well as above, the one true thing everywhere; still even the Upanishads finally fix upon a world of Brahma, and that is above, not below, nor elsewhere; hence the soul must pass the great cosmic potencies that seem to lie on the road from the sublunary regions to Brahma. The K[=a]ush[=i]taki Upanishad (1. 2. 3) arranges that all who leave this world first go to the moon, the moon being the door of the world of light. The moon asks certain theosophic questions; he alone who can answer them is considered sufficiently emancipated to advance to the world of Brahma. He who cannot--alas!--is born again as worm or as fly; as fish or as fowl; as lion or as boar; as bull or tiger or man; or as something else--any old thing, as we should say--in this place or in that place, according to the quality of his works and the degree of his knowledge; that is, in accordance with the doctrine of **Karma**. Similarly the M[=a]itri Upanishad (vi. 38) sketches salvation as follows: When a mortal no longer approves of wrath, and ponders the true wish, he penetrates the veil that encloses the Brahma, breaks through the concentric circles of sun, moon, fire, etc., that occupy the ether. Only then does he behold the supreme thing that is founded upon its own greatness only. And now the Ch[=a]ndogya Upanishad (viii. 13) has the same idea, mentioning both moon and sun by their ancient names and in their capacity as dogs of Yama. The soul of the aspirant for fusion with Brahma resorts purgatorio-fashion alternately to Cy[=a]ma (the moon-dog) and Cabala (the sun-dog): "From Cy[=a]ma (the moon) do I resort to Cabala (the sun); from Cabala to Cy[=a]ma. Shaking off sin, as a steed shakes off (the loose hair of) its mane, as the moon frees itself from the maw of R[=a]hu, the demon of eclipse, casting aside my body, my real self delivered, do I enter into the uncreated world of Brahma."[13]

ANALYSIS OF THE MYTH.

Hindu mythology is famous for what I should like to hear called arrested personification, or arrested anthropomorphism. More than elsewhere mythic figures seem here to cling to the dear memories of their birth and youth. This is due in part to the unequaled impressiveness of nature in India; in part to the dogged schematism of the Hindu mind, which dislikes to let go of any part of a thing from the beginning to end. On the one hand, their constant, almost too rhythmic resort to nature in their poetry, and on the other, their Ved[=a]nta philosophy, or for that matter their *Ars amatoria* (K[=a]mac[=a]stra), the latter worked out with painstaking and undignified detail, illustrate the two points. Hence we find here a situation which is familiar enough in the Veda, but scarcely and rarely exhibited in other mythological fields. Dogs, the two dogs of Yama are, but yet, too, sun and moon. It is quite surprising how well the attributes of things so different keep on fitting them both well enough. The color and brightness of the sun jumps with the fixed epithet, "spotted," of the sun-dog Cabala; the moon-dog is black (Cy[=a]ma or Cy[=a]va). Sun and moon, as they move across the sky, are the natural messengers of Yama, seated on high in the abode of the blessed, but Yama is after all death, and death hounds us all. Epithets like "man-beholding," or "guarding the way," suit neutrally both conceptions. Above all, the earliest statements about Yama's dogs are relieved of their inconsistencies. On the one hand the exhortation to the dead to run past the two dogs in order to get to heaven, suits the idea of the heavenly dogs who are coursing across the sky. On the other hand, by an easy, though quite contrary, change of mental position, the same two heavenly dogs are the guides who guard the way and look upon men favorably; hence they are ordered by Yama to take charge of the dead and to furnish them such health and prosperity as the shades happen to have use for. Again, by an equally simple shift of position, sun and moon move among men as the messengers of death; by night and by day men perish, while these heavenly bodies alternate in their presence among men.[14] Hence a text of the Veda can say in a similar mood: "May Day and Night procure for us long life" (House-book of [=A]cval[=a]yana, ii. 4. 14). Conversely it is a commonplace of the Veda to say that day and night destroy the lives of men. One text says that, "day and night are the encircling arms of death" (Br[=a]hmana of the K[=a]ush[=i]takin, ii. 9). Another, more explicitly, "the year is death"; by means of day and night does it destroy the life of mortals (Catapatha-Br[=a]hmana, x. 4. 3. 1). He who wishes to be released from the grim grip of day and night sacrifices (symbolically) white and black rice, and pronounces the words: "Hail to Day; hail to Night; hail to Release" (Br[=a]hmana of the T[=a]ittiriya, iii. 1. 6. 2). Who does not remember in this connection the parable widely current in the Orient, in which two rats, one white, the other black, gnaw alternately, but without let-up, the plant or tree of life?[15]

THE CERBERI IN THE NORSE MYTH.

Norse mythology also contains certain animal pairs which seem to reflect the two dualities, sun and moon, and day and night. There is here no certainty as to detail; the Norse myth is advanced and congealed, if not spurious, as Professor Bugge and his school would have us believe. At the feet of Odin lie his two wolves, Geri and Freki, "Greedy" and "Voracious." They hurl themselves across the lands when peace is broken. Who shall say that they are to be entirely dissociated from Yama's two dogs of death? The virgin Mengloedh sleeps in her wonderful castle on the mountain called Hyfja, guarded by the two dogs Geri and Gifr, "Greedy" and "Violent," who take turns in watching; only alternately may they sleep as they watch the Hyfja mountain. "One sleeps by night, the other by day, and thus no one may enter" (Fioelsvinnsmal, 16). It is not necessary to suppose any direct connection between this fable and the Vedic myth, but the root of the thought, no matter from how great a distance it may have come, and how completely it may have been worked over by the Norse skald, is, after all, alternating sun and moon and their partners, day and night.

CERBERUS IN THE PERSIAN AVESTA.

No reasonable student of mythology will demand of a myth so clearly destined for fructification an everlasting virginal inviolateness. From the start almost the two dogs of Yama are the brood of Saram[=a]. Why? Saram[=a] is the female messenger of the gods, at the root identical with Hermes or Hermeias; she is therefore the predestined mother of those other messengers, the two four-eyed dogs of Yama. And as the latter are her litter the myth becomes retroactive; she herself is fancied later on as a four-eyed bitch (Atharva-Veda, iv. 20. 7). Similarly the epithet "broad-nosed" stands not in need of mythic interpretation, as soon as it has become a question of life-hunting dogs. Elusive and vague, I confess, is the persistent and important attribute "four-eyed." This touch is both old and widespread. The *Avesta*, the bible of the ancient Iranians, has reduced the Cerberus myth to stunted rudiments. In *Vendidad*, xiii. 8. 9, the killing of dogs is forbidden, because the soul of the slayer "when passing to the other world, shall fly amid louder howling and fiercer pursuit than the sheep does when the wolf rushes upon it in the lofty forest. No soul will come and meet his departing soul and help it through the howls and pursuit in the other world; nor will the dogs that keep the Cinvad bridge (the bridge to paradise) help his departing soul through the howls and pursuit in the other world." The *Avesta* also conceives this dog to be four-eyed. When a man dies, as soon as the soul has parted from the body, the evil one, the corpse-devil (Druj Nasu), from the regions of hell, falls upon the dead. Whoever henceforth touches the corpse becomes unclean, and makes unclean whomsoever he touches. The devil is expelled from the dead by means of the "look of the dog": a "four-eyed dog" is brought near the body and is made to look at the dead; as soon as he has done so the devil flees back to hell (Vendidad, vii. 7; viii. 41). It is not easy to fetch from a mythological hell mythological monsters for casual purposes, especially as men are always engaged in dying upon the earth. Herakles is the only one who, one single time, performed this notable "stunt." So the Parsis, being at a loss to find four-eyed dogs, interpret the name as meaning a dog with two spots over the eyes. Curiously enough the Hindu scholiasts also regularly interpret the term "four-eyed" in exactly the same way, "with spots over the eyes." And the Vedic ritual in its turn has occasion to realize the mythological four-eyed dog in practice. The horse, at the horse-sacrifice, must take a bath for consecration to the holy end to which it is put. It must also be guarded against hostile influences. A low-caste man brings a four-eyed dog--here obviously the symbol of the hostile powers--kills him with a club, and afterwards places him under the feet of the horse. It is scarcely necessary to state that this is a dog with spots over his eyes, and that he is a symbol of Cerberus.[16]

THE TERM "FOUR-EYED."

The epithet "four-eyed" may possibly contain a tentative coagulation of the two dogs in one. The capacity of the two dogs to see both by day (the sun) and by night (the moon) may have given the myth a slight start into the direction of the two-headed Greek Cerberus. But there is the alternate possibility that four-eyed is but a figure of speech for "sharp-sighted," especially as I have shown elsewhere that the parallel expression "to run with four feet" is a Vedic figure of speech for "swift of foot."[17] Certainly the god Agni, "Fire," is once in the *Rig-Veda* (i. 31. 13) called "four-eyed," which can only mean "sharp-sighted."

THE DUAL CABAL[=A]U.

The two dogs of Yama derive their proper names from their color epithets. The passages above make it clear that Cy[=a]ma (rarely Cy[=a]va), "the black," is the moon dog, and that Cabala, "the spotted, or brindled," is the sun dog. In one early passage (Rig-Veda, x. 14. 10) both dogs are named in the dual as Cabal[=a]u. But for a certain Vedic usage one might think that "the two spotted ones" was their earliest designation. The usage referred to is the eliptic dual: a close or natural pair, each member of which suggests the other, may be expressed through the dual of one of them, as when either m[=a]tar[=a]u or pitar[=a]u, literally, "the two mothers," and "the two fathers," each mean "the two parents."[18] From this we may conclude that Cabal[=a]u means really Cabala and Cy[=a]ma, and not the two Cabalas, that is, "the two spotted ones."

IS CABALAS = [Greek: Kerberos]?

More than a hundred years ago the Anglo-Indian Wilford, in the *Asiatick Researches*, iii., page 409, wrote: "Yama, the regent of hell, has two dogs, according to the Pur[=a]nas; one of them named Cerbura, or varied; the other Syama, or black." He then compares Cerbura with Kerberos, of course. The form Cerbura he obtained from his consulting Pandit, who explained the name Cabala by the Sanskrit word **karbura** "variegated," a regular gloss of the Hindu scholiasts.

About fifty years later a number of distinguished scholars of the past generation, Max Mueller, Albrecht Weber, and Theodor Benfey, compared the word Cabala with Greek [Greek: Kerberos] (rarely [Greek: Kerbelos]), but, since then, this identification has been assailed in numerous quarters with some degree of heat, because it suffers from a slight phonetic difficulty. One need but remember the swift changes which the name of Apollo passes through in the mouths of the Greeks-- [Greek: Apollon], [Greek: Apellon], [Greek: Appellon], [Greek: Apeilon], [Greek: Aploun][19]--to realize that it is useless to demand strict phonetic conservation of mythic proper names. The nominative Cabalas, translated sound for sound into Greek, yields [Greek: Keberos], [Greek: Kebelos]; *vice versa*, [Greek: Kerberos?] translated sound for sound into Vedic Sanskrit yields Calbalas, or perhaps, dialectically, Cabbalas. It is a sober view that considers it rather surprising that the two languages have not manipulated their respective versions of the word so as to increase still further the phonetic distance between them. Certainly the burden is now to prove that the identification is to be rejected, and, I think, that the soundest linguistic science will refuse ultimately to consider the phonetic discrepancy between the two words as a matter of serious import.

But whether the names Cabalas and Kerberos are identical or not, the myth itself is the thing. The explanation which we have coaxed step by step from the texts of the Veda imparts to the myth a definite character: it is no longer a dark and uncertain touch in the troubled visions of hell, but an uncommonly lucid treatment of an important cosmic phenomenon. Sun and moon course across the sky: beyond is the abode of light and the blessed. The coursers are at one moment regarded as barring the way to heaven; at another as outposts who may guide the soul to heaven. In yet another mood, as they constantly, day by day, look down upon the race of men, dying day by day, they are regarded as picking daily candidates for the final journey. In due time Yama and his heaven are degraded to a mere Pluto and hell; then the terrible character of the two dogs is all that can be left to them. And the two dogs blend into a unit variously, either a four-eyed Parsi dog, or a two-headed--finally a plural-headed--Kerberos.

OTHER DOGS OF HELL.

The peace of mind of one or the other reader is likely to be disturbed by the appearance of a hell-dog here and there among peoples outside of the Indo-European (Aryan) family. So, e. g., I. G. Mueller, in his **Geschichte der Americanischen Urreligionen**, second edition, p. 88, mentions a dog who threatens to swallow the souls in their passage of the river of hell. There was a custom among the Mordwines to put a club into the coffin with the corpse, to enable him to drive away the watch-dogs at the gate of the nether world.[20] The Mordwines, however, have borrowed much of their mythology from the Iranians. The Hurons and Iroquois told the early missionaries that after death the soul must cross a deep and swift river on a bridge formed by a single slender tree, where it had to defend itself against the attacks of a dog.[21] No sane ethnologist or philologer will insist that all these conceptions are related **genetically**, that there is nothing accidental in the repetition of the idea. The dog is prominent in animal mythology; one of his functions is to watch. It is quite possible, nay likely, that a dog, pure and simple, has strayed occasionally into this sphere of conceptions without any further organic meaning--simply as a baying, hostile watch-dog. But we cannot prove anything by an ignorant **non possumus**; the conception **may**, even if we cannot say **must**, after all in each case, have been derived from essentially the same source: the dead journeying upward to heaven interfered with by a coursing heavenly body, the sun or the moon, or both. Anyhow, the organic quality of the Indo-European, or at least the Hindu myth makes it guide and philosopher. From dual sun and moon coursing across the sky to the two hell-hounds, each step of development is no less clear than from Zeus pater, "Father Sky," to breezy Jove, the gentleman about town with his escapades and amours. To reverse the process, to imagine that the Hindus started with two visionary dogs and finally identified them with sun and moon--that is as easy and natural as it is for a river to flow up the hill back to its source.

MAX MUeLLER'S CERBERUS.

The rudiment of the present essay in Comparative Mythology was published by the writer some years ago in a learned journal, under the title, "The two dogs of Yama in a new role."[22] My late lamented friend, Max Mueller, the gifted writer who knew best of all men how to rivet the attention of the cultivated public upon questions of this sort, did me the honor to notice my proposition in an article in the **London Academy** of August 13, 1892 (number 1058, page 134-5), entitled "Professor Bloomfield's Contributions to the Interpretation of the Veda." In this article he seems to try to establish a certain similarity between his conception of the Kerberos myth and my own. This similarity seems to me to be entirely illusory. Professor Mueller's own last words on the subject in the Preface of his **Contributions to the Science of Mythology** (p. xvi.), will make clear the difference between our views. He identifies, as he always has identified, Kerberos with the Vedic stem *carvara*, from which is derived carvar[=i], "night." To quote his own words: "The germ of the idea ... must be discovered in that nocturnal darkness, that c[=a]rvaram tamas, which native mythologists in India had not yet quite forgotten in post-Vedic times." With such a view my own has not the least point of contact. Cabala, the name of one of the dogs, means "spotted, bright"; it is the name of the sun-dog; it is quite the opposite of the c[=a]rvaram tamas. The name of the moon-dog, and, by transfer, the dog of the night, is Cy[=a]ma or Cy[=a]va "black," not Cabala, nor Carvara. The association of the two dogs with day and night is the association of sun and moon with their respective diurnal divisions, and nothing more. Of Cimmerian gloom there can be nothing in the myth primarily, because it deals at the beginning with heaven, and not with hell; with an auspicious, and not a gloomy, vision of life after death.

CERBERUS AND COMPARATIVE MYTHOLOGY.

In conclusion I would draw the attention of those scholars, writers, and publicists that have declared bankruptcy against the methods and results of Comparative Mythology to the present attempt to establish an Indo-European naturalistic myth. I would ask them to consider, in the light of the Veda, that it is probable that the early notions of future life turn to the visible heaven with its sun and moon, rather than to the topographically unstable and elusive caves and gullies that lead to a wide-gated Hades. In heaven, therefore, and not in hell, is the likely breeding spot of the Cerberus myth. On the way to heaven there is but one pair that can have shaped itself reasonably in the minds of primitive observers into a pair of Cerberi. Sun and moon, the Veda declares, are the Cerberi. In due time, and by gradual stages, the heaven myth became a hell myth. The Vedic seers had no Pluto, no Hades, no Styx, and no Charon; yet they had the pair of dogs. Now when Yama and his heaven become Pluto and hell, then, and only then, Yama's dogs are on a plane with the three-headed, or two-headed, Greek Kerberos. Is it not likely that the chthonic hell visions of the Greeks were also preceded by heavenly visions, and that Kerberos originally sprang from heaven? Consider, too, the breadth and the persistence of these ideas, their simple background, and their natural transition from one feature to another in the myth of Cerberus; that is, the notions of sun and moon (day and night) in their relation to the precarious life of man upon the earth, his death, and his future life. For my part, I do not believe that the honest critics of the methods and results of Comparative Mythology, though they have been made justly suspicious by the many failures in this field, will ever successfully "run past, straightway, the two four-eyed dogs, the spotted and the dark, the Cabal[=a]u, the brood of Saram[=a]."

NOTES:

[1] *Iliad* viii. 368; *Odyssey* xi. 623.

[2] *Theogony*, 311 ff.; cf. also 769 ff.

[3] *Republic*, 588 C.

[4] Baumeister, volume I., page 620 (figure 690).

[5] Baumeister, volume I., page 379 (figure 415).

[6] Baumeister, volume I., page 653 (figure 721).

[7] Baumeister, volume I., page 663 (figure 730). See the Frontispiece and its explanation.

[8] *American Journal of Archaeology*, volume XI., page 14 (figure 12, page 15).

[9] *Custos opaci pervigil regni canis.* Seneca.

[10] *Inferno*, Canto vi., 13 ff.

[11] See p. 99 of the Teubner edition of his writings.

[12] Fulgentius, Liber I., Fabula VI., de Tricerbero, p. 20 of the Teubner edition.

[13] Both Cankara, the great Hindu theologian and commentator of the Upanishads, as well as all modern interpreters of the Upanishads, have failed to see the sense of this passage.

[14] Cf. the notion of the sun as the "highest death" in T[=a]ittir[=i]va Br[=a]hmana, i. 8. 4.

[15] See Ernst Kuhn, Festgruss an Otto von Boehtlingk, page 68 ff.

[16] Similar notions in Russia and Russian Asia are reported by Wsevolod Miller, Atti del iv. *Congresso Internazionale degli Orientalisti*, vol. ii. p. 43; and by Casartelli, *Babylonian and Oriental Record*, iv. 266 ff. They are most likely derived from Iranian sources.

[17] See *American Journal of Philology*, vol. XI., p. 355.

[18] Similarly in Greek [Greek: Aiante] means Ajax and Teukros; see Delbrueck, *Vergleichende Syntax*, i. 137.

[19] See Usener, Goetternamen, p. 303 ff.

[20] Max Mueller, ***Contributions to the Science of Mythology***, p. 240.

[21] Brinton, ***The Myths of the New World***. Second Edition, p. 265.

[22] Presented to the American Oriental Society at its meeting May 5, 1891; and printed in its Journal, Vol. XV., pp. 163 ff.

The Codes Of Hammurabi And Moses
W. W. Davies

QTY

The discovery of the Hammurabi Code is one of the greatest achievements of archaeology, and is of paramount interest, not only to the student of the Bible, but also to all those interested in ancient history...

Religion   **ISBN:** *1-59462-338-4*   **Pages:132**
MSRP $12.95

The Theory of Moral Sentiments
Adam Smith

QTY

This work from 1749. contains original theories of conscience amd moral judgment and it is the foundation for systemof morals.

Philosophy **ISBN:** *1-59462-777-0*   **Pages:536**
MSRP $19.95

Jessica's First Prayer
Hesba Stretton

QTY

In a screened and secluded corner of one of the many railway-bridges which span the streets of London there could be seen a few years ago, from five o'clock every morning until half past eight, a tidily set-out coffee-stall, consisting of a trestle and board, upon which stood two large tin cans, with a small fire of charcoal burning under each so as to keep the coffee boiling during the early hours of the morning when the work-people were thronging into the city on their way to their daily toil...

Childrens   **ISBN:** *1-59462-373-2*   **Pages:84**
MSRP $9.95

My Life and Work
Henry Ford

QTY

Henry Ford revolutionized the world with his implementation of mass production for the Model T automobile. Gain valuable business insight into his life and work with his own auto-biography... "We have only started on our development of our country we have not as yet, with all our talk of wonderful progress, done more than scratch the surface. The progress has been wonderful enough but..."

Biographies/ **ISBN:** *1-59462-198-5*   **Pages:300**
MSRP $21.95

The Art of Cross-Examination
Francis Wellman

QTY

I presume it is the experience of every author, after his first book is published upon an important subject, to be almost overwhelmed with a wealth of ideas and illustrations which could readily have been included in his book, and which to his own mind, at least, seem to make a second edition inevitable. Such certainly was the case with me; and when the first edition had reached its sixth impression in five months, I rejoiced to learn that it seemed to my publishers that the book had met with a sufficiently favorable reception to justify a second and considerably enlarged edition. ..

Reference   ISBN: *1-59462-647-2*

Pages:412

MSRP $19.95

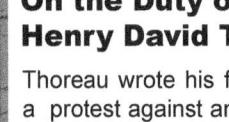

On the Duty of Civil Disobedience
Henry David Thoreau

QTY

Thoreau wrote his famous essay, On the Duty of Civil Disobedience, as a protest against an unjust but popular war and the immoral but popular institution of slave-owning. He did more than write—he declined to pay his taxes,   and was hauled off to gaol in consequence. Who can say how much this refusal of his hastened the end of the war and of slavery ?

Law   ISBN: *1-59462-747-9*

Pages:48

MSRP $7.45

Dream Psychology Psychoanalysis for Beginners
Sigmund Freud

QTY

Sigmund Freud, born Sigismund Schlomo Freud (May 6, 1856 - September 23, 1939), was a Jewish-Austrian neurologist and psychiatrist who co-founded the psychoanalytic school of psychology. Freud is best known for his theories of the unconscious mind, especially involving the mechanism of repression; his redefinition of sexual desire as mobile and directed towards a wide variety of objects; and his therapeutic techniques, especially his understanding of transference in the therapeutic relationship and the presumed value of dreams as sources of insight into unconscious desires.

Psychology   ISBN: *1-59462-905-6*

Pages:196

MSRP $15.45

The Miracle of Right Thought
Orison Swett Marden

QTY

Believe with all of your heart that you will do what you were made to do. When the mind has once formed the habit of holding cheerful, happy, prosperous pictures, it will not be easy to form the opposite habit. It does not matter how improbable or how far away this realization may see, or how dark the prospects may be, if we visualize them as best we can, as vividly as possible, hold tenaciously to them and vigorously struggle to attain them, they will gradually become actualized, realized in the life. But a desire, a longing without endeavor, a yearning abandoned or held indifferently will vanish without realization.

Self Help   ISBN: *1-59462-644-8*

Pages:360

MSRP $25.45

The Rosicrucian Cosmo-Conception Mystic Christianity by *Max Heindel* ISBN: *1-59462-188-8* **$38.95**
The Rosicrucian Cosmo-conception is not dogmatic, neither does it appeal to any other authority than the reason of the student. It is: not controversial, but is: sent forth in the, hope that it may help to clear... New Age/Religion Pages 646

Abandonment To Divine Providence by *Jean-Pierre de Caussade* ISBN: *1-59462-228-0* **$25.95**
"The Rev. Jean Pierre de Caussade was one of the most remarkable spiritual writers of the Society of Jesus in France in the 18th Century. His death took place at Toulouse in 1751. His works have gone through many editions and have been republished... Inspirational/Religion Pages 400

Mental Chemistry by *Charles Haanel* ISBN: *1-59462-192-5* **$23.95**
Mental Chemistry allows the change of material conditions by combining and appropriately utilizing the power of the mind. Much like applied chemistry creates something new and unique out of careful combinations of chemicals the mastery of mental chemistry... New Age Pages 354

The Letters of Robert Browning and Elizabeth Barret Barrett 1845-1846 vol II ISBN: *1-59462-193-4* **$35.95**
by *Robert Browning* and *Elizabeth Barrett* Biographies Pages 596

Gleanings In Genesis (volume I) by *Arthur W. Pink* ISBN: *1-59462-130-6* **$27.45**
Appropriately has Genesis been termed "the seed plot of the Bible" for in it we have, in germ form, almost all of the great doctrines which are afterwards fully developed in the books of Scripture which follow... Religion/Inspirational Pages 420

The Master Key by *L. W. de Laurence* ISBN: *1-59462-001-6* **$30.95**
In no branch of human knowledge has there been a more lively increase of the spirit of research during the past few years than in the study of Psychology, Concentration and Mental Discipline. The requests for authentic lessons in Thought Control, Mental Discipline and... New Age/Business Pages 422

The Lesser Key Of Solomon Goetia by *L. W. de Laurence* ISBN: *1-59462-092-X* **$9.95**
This translation of the first book of the "Lernegton" which is now for the first time made accessible to students of Talismanic Magic was done, after careful collation and edition, from numerous Ancient Manuscripts in Hebrew, Latin, and French... New Age/Occult Pages 92

Rubaiyat Of Omar Khayyam by *Edward Fitzgerald* ISBN:*1-59462-332-5* **$13.95**
Edward Fitzgerald, whom the world has already learned, in spite of his own efforts to remain within the shadow of anonymity, to look upon as one of the rarest poets of the century, was born at Bredfield, in Suffolk, on the 31st of March, 1809. He was the third son of John Purcell... Music Pages 172

Ancient Law by *Henry Maine* ISBN: *1-59462-128-4* **$29.95**
The chief object of the following pages is to indicate some of the earliest ideas of mankind, as they are reflected in Ancient Law, and to point out the relation of those ideas to modern thought. Religion/History Pages 452

Far-Away Stories by *William J. Locke* ISBN: *1-59462-129-2* **$19.45**
"Good wine needs no bush", but a collection of mixed vintages does. And this book is just such a collection. Some of the stories I do not want to remain buried for ever in the museum files of dead magazine-numbers an author's not unpardonable vanity..." Fiction Pages 272

Life of David Crockett by *David Crockett* ISBN: *1-59462-250-7* **$27.45**
"Colonel David Crockett was one of the most remarkable men of the times in which he lived. Born in humble life, but gifted with a strong will, an indomitable courage, and unremitting perseverance... Biographies/New Age Pages 424

Lip-Reading by *Edward Nitchie* ISBN: *1-59462-206-X* **$25.95**
Edward B. Nitchie, founder of the New York School for the Hard of Hearing, now the Nitchie School of Lip-Reading, Inc, wrote "LIP-READING Principles and Practice". The development and perfecting of this meritorious work on lip-reading was an undertaking... How-to Pages 400

A Handbook of Suggestive Therapeutics, Applied Hypnotism, Psychic Science ISBN: *1-59462-214-0* **$24.95**
by *Henry Munro* Health/New Age/Health/Self-help Pages 376

A Doll's House: and Two Other Plays by *Henrik Ibsen* ISBN: *1-59462-112-8* **$19.95**
Henrik Ibsen created this classic when in revolutionary 1848 Rome. Introducing some striking concepts in playwriting for the realist genre, this play has been studied the world over. Fiction/Classics/Plays 308

The Light of Asia by *sir Edwin Arnold* ISBN: *1-59462-204-3* **$13.95**
In this poetic masterpiece, Edwin Arnold describes the life and teachings of Buddha. The man who was to become known as Buddha to the world was born as Prince Gautama of India but he rejected the worldly riches and abandoned the reigns of power when... Religion/History/Biographies Pages 170

The Complete Works of Guy de Maupassant by *Guy de Maupassant* ISBN: *1-59462-157-8* **$16.95**
"For days and days, nights and nights, I had dreamed of that first kiss which was to consecrate our engagement, and I knew not on what spot I should put my lips..." Fiction/Classics Pages 240

The Art of Cross-Examination by *Francis L. Wellman* ISBN: *1-59462-309-0* **$26.95**
Written by a renowned trial lawyer, Wellman imparts his experience and uses case studies to explain how to use psychology to extract desired information through questioning. How-to/Science/Reference Pages 408

Answered or Unanswered? by *Louisa Vaughan* ISBN: *1-59462-248-5* **$10.95**
Miracles of Faith in China Religion Pages 112

The Edinburgh Lectures on Mental Science (1909) by *Thomas* ISBN: *1-59462-008-3* **$11.95**
This book contains the substance of a course of lectures recently given by the writer in the Queen Street Hall, Edinburgh. Its purpose is to indicate the Natural Principles governing the relation between Mental Action and Material Conditions... New Age/Psychology Pages 148

Ayesha by *H. Rider Haggard* ISBN: *1-59462-301-5* **$24.95**
Verily and indeed it is the unexpected that happens! Probably if there was one person upon the earth from whom the Editor of this, and of a certain previous history, did not expect to hear again... Classics Pages 380

Ayala's Angel by *Anthony Trollope* ISBN: *1-59462-352-X* **$29.95**
The two girls were both pretty, but Lucy who was twenty-one who supposed to be simple and comparatively unattractive, whereas Ayala was credited, as her Bombwhat romantic name might show, with poetic charm and a taste for romance. Ayala when her father died was nineteen... Fiction Pages 484

The American Commonwealth by *James Bryce* ISBN: *1-59462-286-8* **$34.45**
An interpretation of American democratic political theory. It examines political mechanics and society from the perspective of Scotsman James Bryce Politics Pages 572

Stories of the Pilgrims by *Margaret P. Pumphrey* ISBN: *1-59462-116-0* **$17.95**
This book explores pilgrims religious oppression in England as well as their escape to Holland and eventual crossing to America on the Mayflower, and their early days in New England... History Pages 268

www.bookjungle.com *email: sales@bookjungle.com fax: 630-214-0564 mail: Book Jungle PO Box 2226 Champaign, IL 61825*

QTY

The Fasting Cure *by Sinclair Upton* ISBN: *1-59462-222-1* **$13.95**
In the Cosmopolitan Magazine for May, 1910, and in the Contemporary Review (London) for April, 1910, I published an article dealing with my experiences in fasting. I have written a great many magazine articles, but never one which attracted so much attention... New Age/Self Help/Health Pages 164

Hebrew Astrology *by Sepharial* ISBN: *1-59462-308-2* **$13.45**
In these days of advanced thinking it is a matter of common observation that we have left many of the old landmarks behind and that we are now pressing forward to greater heights and to a wider horizon than that which represented the mind-content of our progenitors... Astrology Pages 144

Thought Vibration or The Law of Attraction in the Thought World ISBN: *1-59462-127-6* **$12.95**
by William Walker Atkinson Psychology/Religion Pages 144

Optimism *by Helen Keller* ISBN: *1-59462-108-X* **$15.95**
Helen Keller was blind, deaf, and mute since 19 months old, yet famously learned how to overcome these handicaps, communicate with the world, and spread her lectures promoting optimism. An inspiring read for everyone... Biographies/Inspirational Pages 84

Sara Crewe *by Frances Burnett* ISBN: *1-59462-360-0* **$9.45**
In the first place, Miss Minchin lived in London. Her home was a large, dull, tall one, in a large, dull square, where all the houses were alike, and all the sparrows were alike, and where all the door-knockers made the same heavy sound... Childrens/Classic Pages 88

The Autobiography of Benjamin Franklin *by Benjamin Franklin* ISBN: *1-59462-135-7* **$24.95**
The Autobiography of Benjamin Franklin has probably been more extensively read than any other American historical work, and no other book of its kind has had such ups and downs of fortune. Franklin lived for many years in England, where he was agent... Biographies/History Pages 332

Name	
Email	
Telephone	
Address	
City, State ZIP	

☐ **Credit Card**   ☐ **Check / Money Order**

Credit Card Number	
Expiration Date	
Signature	

Please Mail to: Book Jungle
PO Box 2226
Champaign, IL 61825
or Fax to: 630-214-0564

ORDERING INFORMATION

web*: www.bookjungle.com*
email*: sales@bookjungle.com*
fax*: 630-214-0564*
mail*: Book Jungle PO Box 2226 Champaign, IL 61825*
or PayPal *to sales@bookjungle.com*

Please contact us for bulk discounts

DIRECT-ORDER TERMS

**20% Discount if You Order
Two or More Books**
Free Domestic Shipping!
Accepted: Master Card, Visa,
Discover, American Express

www.ingramcontent.com/pod-product-compliance
Lightning Source LLC
Chambersburg PA
CBHW081203170626
46813CB00009B/3300